Every Child Has a Story
Before Bedtime

THE ASTRONAUT'S VISIT

Copyright © 2014 by Beverly Jones-Durr
Published by: Gifted Genie Publishing

The sun was bright. There was a slight breeze flowing into Stevie's room. Stevie was awake, but lying in bed thinking. He thought about a lot of things, but this morning spaceships were on his mind. Stevie has dreams of becoming an engineer who builds rockets and the fastest race cars ever! If anyone was going to do it, it would be him. It was a school day. He threw back the covers and hopped out of bed. School was one of his favorite places. He loved learning new things. "I can't be late for school," he said as he entered the bathroom and closed the door.

After a few minutes, Stevie exited the bathroom fully dressed. He made his bed. Grabbing his backpack, he headed for the kitchen. His mom was already working on breakfast. "Would you like eggs this morning Stevie or would you prefer cereal?" asked his mom. Stevie's mom made the best eggs. But this morning Stevie didn't have time. "I'll have cereal today Mom," answered Stevie. He finished his cereal, kissed his mom and headed out the door to catch the bus.

Arriving at school, Stevie headed straight to his locker to get the book he needed for his first class, Science. Stevie loved Science class. It was one of his favorite classes. Gathering what he needed, he rushed to class. Upon entering the classroom, Stevie noticed the chairs and desks had been rearranged. They were arranged in a semi-circle and all facing the projection screen. Stevie took a seat in the center directly in front of the projection screen.

The rest of the class entered the room. They eventually found their seats and settled down. "Where is the teacher?" asked one of the students. "I don't know," responded another. "But we should sit quietly and wait for her." After about 5 minutes, the teacher entered the classroom. Following her was a man carrying a space helmet. Stevie sat straight up in his seat. He was very curious now to know who this stranger was. "Good morning class. Thank you for being so well behaved during my absence. I have a super surprise for you today. I'd like to introduce Retired Colonel Benjamin Alvin Drew, NASA Astronaut." Stevie could not believe his eyes. A real NASA astronaut was standing in his classroom!

"**H**ello class. I'm honored to be here today and talk with you about the space program. I look forward to answering all your questions. But first, I'd like to show you all a short film. It's of an actual rocket launch and a spacewalk. Oh, I almost forgot. You may call me Astronaut Ben."

Astronaut Ben handed a roll of film to the teacher. Loading the film in the projector she instructed the class to settle down. "Astronaut Ben has brought us a great film. Let's get started," she said as the movie begin to play. Astronaut Ben turned off the lights.

Stevie sat quietly in his seat. Every now and again, he'd look over at Astronaut Ben. He simply could not believe he was in the same room with a real astronaut who had been in space. As he watched the film, he imagined himself in the movie. He could picture himself circling the earth and exploring space for new planets and life forms and walking on those new planets.

When the film ended, the teacher turned on the lights. Astronaut Ben grabbed a chair and sat in front of the students. "Now, I know you have questions. Who will be first?" he asked. Everyone started asking questions at once. It was confusing but exciting. "Class, please raise your hand and wait to be called upon," said the teacher. All hands went up in the air. Astronaut Ben selected a student. The student stood and asked, "Did you always want to become an astronaut?" "That's a good question. I watched the space launches with my parents on TV. I knew that when I grew up I wanted to be an astronaut." Astronaut Ben selected another student. "Do you have to like science," asked the student. Astronaut Ben smiled and answered, "I'm afraid so. There's a lot of science in the space program. You need to really love science. It is the foundation for the space program." Astronaut Ben looked right at Stevie. Stevie was sitting on the edge of his seat. His hand was waving anxiously in the air. "You look like you have more than one question young man. Stand up please, tell me a little about yourself," he said to Stevie.

Stevie stood and cleared his throat. Grasping the note pad tightly he replied, "Hi, my name is Stevie Johnson, sir. I love science, race cars, and I want to become an astronaut just like you." "You do? Tell me about your family. Do they encourage you?" he asked. "Well, my mom is a very good mom. She makes sure that I eat healthy foods and that I do my homework. I was once in the local newspaper for my academic performance," said Stevie proudly. "I bet that was a proud moment for you and your family," said Astronaut Ben. "Yes, sir it really was. My aunt Margie took me to the Space and Rocket Center in Huntsville, Alabama. It was awesome! My dad and I race cars on a really huge race track I got for Christmas. My dad really likes those race cars." "It sounds like you have a great family who loves and supports you. Okay, now what's your first question," asked Astronaut Ben. Stevie looked at his note pad and asked, "You must have gone to college. Where did you get your degree?" Astronaut Ben replied, "I actually have four degrees.

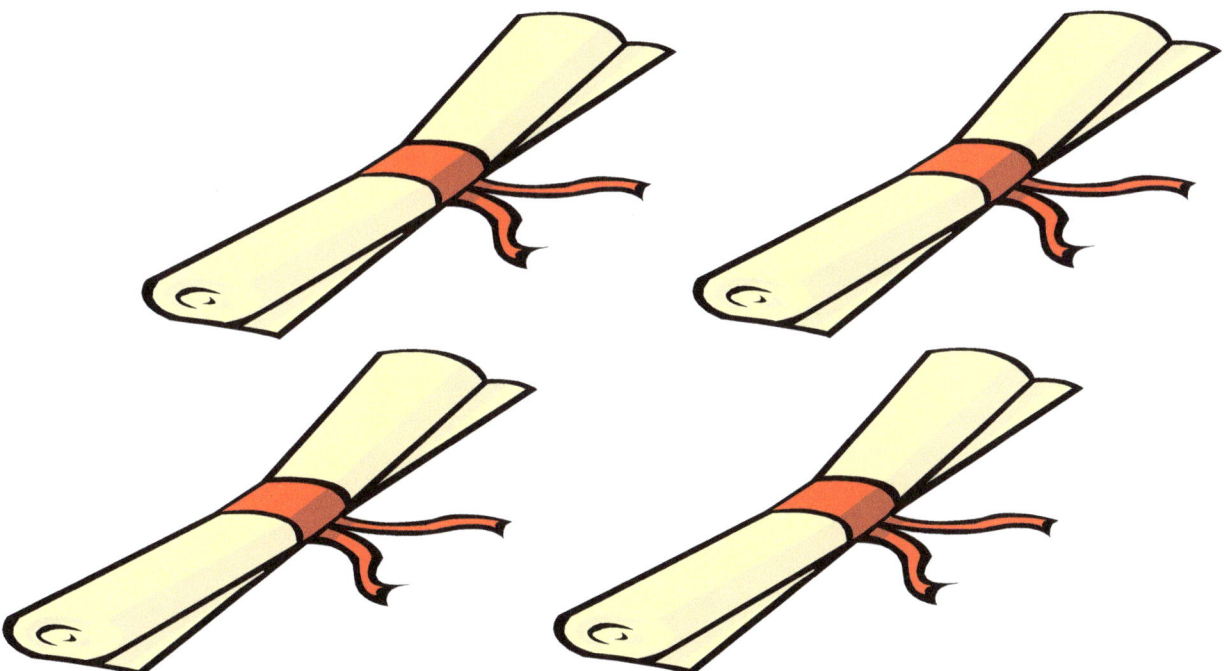

I have two Bachelor's degrees, one in Astronautical Engineering and another in Physics. I received them both from the United States Air Force Academy. I also have two Master's degrees as well. I received a Master's degree in Aerospace Science from Embry Riddle University and a second Master's in Strategic Studies in Political Science from the United States Air Force Academy," he answered proudly. "Wow! That must have taken a lot of school. I'm glad I like school," said Stevie with a smile. "My next question is have you ever piloted a shuttle?" "I have indeed. I piloted the Space Shuttle Discovery in March of 2011. Our mission was to deliver a huge module to the International Space Station. I piloted the 20th flight of the Space Shuttle Endeavour. That mission was to deliver parts, a new gyroscope and a system upgrade to the International Space Station," he answered.

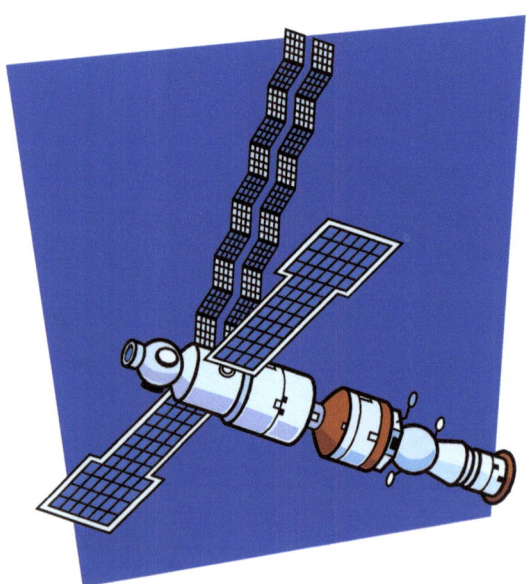

"**W**ere you ever afraid during your mission," asked Stevie. "That's a great question Stevie. Let's talk a little about fear. Fear is a human thing, everybody feels it. I decided to always use fear to my advantage. If I felt fear creeping in I used it as a hint to check all systems thoroughly. It actually helped me to become confident in what I know and what I can do. If you use fear as your reminder to look inside yourself to find the courage to move on, nothing can stop you" answered Astronaut Ben. "Those have been some very good questions, but it is nearly time for the bell to ring. Any final words Astronaut Ben," the teacher asked. Astronaut Ben stood and smiled.

"**I**f you think science doesn't matter much to you, think again. Science affects us all, every day of the year, from the moment we wake up, all day long and through the night. Your digital alarm clock, the weather report, the asphalt your parents drive on, the bus you ride in, your decision to eat a baked potato instead of fries, your cell phone, if you are allowed to have one, the antibiotics that treat your sore throat, the clean water that comes from your faucet and the light that you turn off at the end of the day have all been brought to you courtesy of science. The modern world would not be modern at all without the technology enabled by science. Always do your best work and your parents will be proud. Learn something new every day. It's been an honor for me to be here and I wish you all an incredible life filled with science," said Astronaut Ben. The students and applauded Astronaut Ben as the bell rang for the next class. "Children, please pick up your autographed picture of Astronaut Ben on the desk as you exit the class," said the teacher. Stevie went to his classes the rest of the day, but they were a blur. All he thought about was Astronaut Ben.

Finally, the day was over and the bus was pulling up to Stevie's stop. He hurried off the bus and ran all the way home. When he arrived he ran straight inside. His mom and dad were both home. "How was your day?" asked Stevie's dad. "My day was awesome! We had a real astronaut visit our science class today. He told us a lot about his missions and the space shuttles he flew. We even got an autographed picture of him!" Stevie said with excitement.

"That sounds like you really had an awesome day. Would you like a snack before dinner," asked his mom. "Thank you, but no. I'm going to go to my room. I just want to think about my day. Call me when dinner is ready!" Stevie grabbed his backpack and hurried to his room. He sat at his desk and completed his homework. Once finished, he got his backpack ready for school tomorrow. Feeling a bit tired, Stevie lay down on his bed. He began thinking about Astronaut Ben and all the things he said. Slowly Stevie drifted off to sleep. His dreams were filled with science, astronauts, and piloting a space shuttle. He knew when he grew up he was going to become an astronaut.

Sweet Dreams!

Stevie Johnson, NASA Astronaut.

Lonely Hoops

Copyright © 2014 by Beverly Jones-Durr
Published by: Gifted Genie Publishing

The sun beamed brightly through the window of Mario's room. Mario had plans to shoot hoops with his friends Eric and Rashad today. He leaped out of bed, showered, brushed his teeth, and quickly got dressed. He ran downstairs for breakfast. The kitchen was quiet. Actually, the entire house was quiet. "Hey! Is anyone home?" Mario yelled, but no one answered. On the door of the refrigerator was a note. The note read, "Mario, we will be back in time for dinner. We love you, mom and dad."

"I wonder why they left so early." Mario asked looking at the note. "What could have been so important that mom didn't leave me breakfast?" Mario decided he was much too excited to sit and eat breakfast so he grabbed a breakfast bar, locked the door behind him and set out to find his friends so he could shoot hoops! As Mario approached the pond behind his house he noticed Harold Hippo swimming there. "Hi Harold," said Mario. "Good top of the morning young, Mario. Where are you off to this bright and sunny morning?" asked Harold. "I am looking for my friends so I can shoot some hoops. We have the championship game in a few weeks and I want to be ready. Would you like to join me," asked Mario.

"No, I think I'll stay right here in the pond. It's supposed to be a warm one today," Harold said.

"I'd better go then. Talk with you later," said Mario waving goodbye to Harold.

A short time later, Mario saw a huge frog sitting on a lily pad. He looked a bit upset. "Excuse me, Mr. Frog. Are you okay?" asked Mario. "I am definitely not okay. Someone has stolen my breakfast and I am very upset," answered the frog. "Do you have any idea who might have stolen it?" asked Mario. "If I knew that, I'd have gotten it back," replied the frog. "Well you are welcome to share my breakfast bar if you like," offered Mario reaching into his pocket. "No thanks! Unless it's made out of flies, I don't want it. Just go on and leave me alone. I'll figure something out," the frog said as he hopped away.

Mario continued along the path until he heard splashing and laughter. As he ran to the lake he saw his friends Eric and Rashad rowing downstream.

"Hey guys! Where are you going? Did you forget we are shooting hoops today? We have to be ready for the big game," yelled Mario. "We can't shoot hoops today. We've been invited to join the rowing club at the lake house for lunch," said Eric. "Wait for me! I'll go and get my canoe and join you. We can shoot hoops later," Mario responded. "No time for waiting! We are already late," yelled Rashad as the two rowed up stream and quickly out of sight.

"Stop all that yelling," whispered a voice over by a tree stump. Startled, Mario asked, "Who said that?" "I did," said the voice as a furry face peeped over the tree stump. "My name is Ricky and these are my brothers Paulie and Vito," said Ricky. "What are you three doing over there?" asked Mario. "Isn't it obvious?" answered Vito. "We are hiding." "Hiding from whom?" asked Mario. "We are hiding from our friend Esther. This is a good hiding place, so don't blow it for us. Just move on before she sees you and finds us!" said Paulie. Mario decided to see if he could find someone to shoot hoops with at the Burke farm up the road.

Along the way, Mario saw Mrs. Burke riding her horse Buford. "Hello Mrs. Burke. How are you today?" asked Mario. "No time for talking this morning, Mario. Buford and I have to practice today. He is training for the race next month and I really want to win that ribbon," answered Mrs. Burke as she trotted up the road.

When Mario arrived at the Burke farm, he saw Millie Goat trying on a very pretty dress. "Hi Millie, pretty dress," said

Mario. "Are you going someplace special today?" Millie spun around in her pink dress and answered, "Oh yes, I have a party to attend today and I'm trying to decide if pink is a good color for me. What do you think Mario?" asked Millie. "Well, I don't know anything about dresses, but I guess pink is a good color for you," answered Mario. "What time is the party?" asked Mario. "Oh, not until this evening," replied Millie. "Then would you mind helping me practice for the basketball championship? Everyone else seems to be too busy," asked Mario. "I'm sorry, Mario, but a girl has tons to do before making a grand entrance at a party. Now, where did I put those pink heels?" said Millie as she entered the barn.

Mario could smell food cooking from inside the barn. When he entered, sitting in a chair reading a cookbook was Elena pig. Believe it or not, Elena and her sisters Helana and Dana were the best caterers in town! "Hi Elena," said Mario. What's cooking?" Elena seemed a little surprised to see Mario. "Whatever brought you here to see me?" she asked. "Are you serious? I can smell all of my favorite foods coming from this barn. Can I have a sample like last time?" asked Mario. "I'm afraid not," said Elena. "I have a huge party to cater and I cooked just enough food." Feeling pretty disappointed, Mario decided to just go home. He took the long way back so he could just think. Why had his friends avoided him today? He didn't want to run into anymore of his "busy" friends.

By the time Mario arrived at home, the sun was beginning to set. It was almost dinner time so he hurried inside. The house was dark as he entered. Suddenly all the lights came on and Mario heard "Surpise!" Mario saw Eric and Rashad,

Harold Hippo, and Gina Goat in her pink dress with pink heels. His mom Lisa and his dad Mike were also there. "What is going on? Why is everyone here?" he asked. "Well, son, you may have noticed that all your friends were busy today. They were helping your dad and I prepare for your party," answered Mario's mom. "But what's the party for?" asked Mario.

"Mario, you have been so consumed by the basketball championship. Have you forgotten your own birthday?" she asked. "It is my birthday! I did forget!" shouted Mario with glee. "That's why today has been so weird. Everyone here was planning my party. Elena you were cooking for my party today, right?" "Yes, my dear. I know I always let you have samples, and I'm sorry if today I disappointed you," she said. "It's okay, I understand now. But, where is my cake?" Mario asked. "Look behind you," answered Elena.

"Wow! What an awesome cake!" he shouted. Everyone sang happy birthday to Mario. He couldn't wait to cut his cake and talk with his friends. Everyone was there. This was the best ending to what started out being Mario's worst day ever. Everybody danced and had a great time.

"What about the championship?" asked Eric? Mario answered, "Well, there's always tomorrow. Tonight we are going to party!"

Is This Your Elephant?

It's Saturday morning!!! The sun was shining and the sky was blue. Gabriel loves Saturdays. He could play outside all day! His cousins will be over soon to swim in the pool. He just had to clean his room first. This was also a special day for Gabriel. His brother Anthony had arranged for a very special guest. Gabriel has no idea about the surprise guest! Anthony had to go to work after breakfast, but he could hardly wait to hear about Gabe's day.

Gabriel jumped out of bed and quickly went into the bathroom to wash up and brush his teeth. He had to dress quickly so he could begin cleaning his room. He could smell breakfast cooking downstairs. "Gabe are you up?" asked his mom. She had to drag him out of bed on everyday except Saturday.

"Yes, Mom I am up" answered Gabe. Gabe quickly dressed and ran downstairs to eat breakfast. Anthony entered the room. "Good morning" he said as he sat down at the table. "What are you going to do today Gabe?" asked Anthony. "After I clean my room, Beth and Mark are coming over to play and swim in the pool", replied Gabe. Anthony winked at his mom. He had told her about the surprise.

Gabriel finished his breakfast and zipped upstairs to begin cleaning his room. He pulled the covers up on his bed. Threw the pillow on top and picked up his toys. Some didn't fit in the toy box, so Gabe decided to hide them underneath the bed. He hoped that his mom wouldn't looked under the bed! He dusted his furniture and wiped down the sink and tub in his bathroom. Standing in the middle of the room, Gabe said "This looks clean to me". He opened the curtains and looked out the window. Something looked odd. One of the lawn chairs was moved! He ran outside to investigate.

When Gabe got outside, he noticed large circles in the grass. He decided to follow the circles. To Gabe's surprise, standing in his backyard drinking water from the pool was an elephant! The elephant must have really been thirsty because he had drank half the water in the pool. At that moment, Beth came running into the backyard. When she saw the elephant she stopped in her tracks. "Ah, Gabe, there's an elephant in your backyard drinking water from your pool,"she said. "Beth I know about the elephant", replied Gabe.   "Is he your elephant," asked Beth.   "No, this is not my elephant," said Gabe. "Then whose elephant is it," asked Beth.   "I don't know, but I think we should find out. Don't you?"

Gabe and Beth decided to knock on the doors of their neighbors. The elephant followed them trampelling on the neighbors flower bed. Knocking on the door, Gabe couldn't help wondering if he'd be in trouble for the flowers. The door opened and to the nieghbor's surprise, standing on his porch was Gabe, Beth and an elephant. "Good morning sir,"said Gabe. Is this your elephant?" Startled by the question the neighbor said, "Elephant? Of course this is not my elephant. I don't even have a dog! Get that elephant away from here," he yelled as he slammed the door. "Oh well, Guess this is not his elephant. Let's try another neighbor.

"What are you doing with that elephant?" asked Mark. Mark had been to Gabe's house and when he wasn't home decided to look for him. "Is that your elephant Gabe? Cool!" "No, this is not my elephant. I found him drinking out of my pool. Do you want to go along with me and Beth while we look for his owner?" asked Gabe. "Sure," said Mark and the three headed across the street to another nieghbor. As they approached the house they noticed the nieghbor was watering her garden. When she saw the three kids and the elephant she ran inside the house screaming. "What do we do now," asked Gabe. We didn't even get a chance to ask her. I can't keep an elephant. He won't fit in my room, Where would an elephant sleep? What does an elephant eat?" Beth smiled and said, "Maybe he eats hotdogs." "Yuck, I hate hot dogs, said Gabe. I suppose we have to feed him something. Let's go back to my house and try to figure out something." The friends and the elephant headed back to Gabe's house.

When they arrived they saw a big truck parked in the driveway of Gabe's house. There was a man talking to Gabe's Mom. She was looking around as if she had lost something. "What's going on?" asked Gabe. Gabe's mom ran over and said, "There is a wild elephant lose in the neighborhood. I am so glad you, Beth and Mark are alright.   Have you children seen an elephant around here?" Gabe begin jumping up and down happily. "Yes! Yes we saw an elephant and here he is!" But when Gabe turned around, the elephant wasn't there. "He was right here! Where could he be," asked Gabe.   "Let's all look for him, said the man. He really is as gentle as a baby. He won't hurt anyone." Everyone began to look for the elephant. The man looked in the bushes. Beth looked underneath the big truck. Mark even looked in the refrigerator! Gabe's mom looked through her telescope! The elephant didn't seem to be anyplace.

"I found him! I found him!" yelled Gabe from the backyard. To everyone's surprise, standing beside the pool playing in the water was the elephant! All the kids changed into the swimming suits and jumped in the pool.   They played and fed the elephant hot dogs until the sun went down.

At the end of the day the man loaded the elephant into the truck and drove away. "This was a fantastic day," said Gabe. "I think I'm going to take a shower and go to bed". Gabe said goodbye to all his friends. As Gabe was getting into bed, Anthony entered the room. "So, Gabe how did you like your surprise?" "My surprise? What surpise," asked Gabe. "The elephant! Did you like the elephant," asked Anthony. "That was your surprise?" "Yes, it was my surprise. I told mom it was going to be Spiderman because I knew she'd flipped if she knew it was an elephant." "She flipped alright," laughed Gabe. "I guess I ought to tell her the truth now. Wish me luck!" said Anthony knowing how his mom frowned on not being honest. But, seeing how happy his brother was made it all worth it. "Good luck brother and thanks for an awesome surprise! I love you." Anthony smiled and replied, "I love you too Gabe. Goodnight!"

Fairy Cousins

Copyright © 2014 by Beverly Jones-Durr
Published by: Gifted Genie Publishing

It had been a very busy day. Jeniya was very busy cleaning her room and performing her chores around the house. Why is it that I always get stuck doing housework? Doesn't everyone know that I come from royalty? One of these days I'm really going to show them, thought Jeniya." When Jeniya was finished, her mother allowed her to call her cousin Breezy. They both dreamed and believed in their hearts that they were destined to be Fairy Princesses. "Hello, Breezy, this is Jeniya. What you doing tonight?" Frowning Breezy replies, "The usual, cleaning my room and getting ready for bed." "Well, today in school I overheard some girls talking to my friend Angel. Angel said that there is a special place where girls can go to learn how to become a fairy princess," whispered Jeniya. "Really?" asked Breezy with excitement. I have dreamed of being a fairy princess for so long." "So have I, responded Janiya. I think we should go there Breezy and I also think we should go there tonight! If we have any chance of making our dream come true, we really need to go right now." Curious, Breezy responded, "How are we supposed to get there? We are both too young to drive. And we have no money. Won't our families be angry if they find out we have gone away," asked Breezy. Jeniya smiled, "they won't even know we are gone. Angel gave me magic words so when we use them our family will sleep until we return," said Jeniya. "Are you sure that's going to be okay," asked Breezy. "It worked for Angel. She says she's an official fairy princess. I think it's worth a try," replied Jeniya. "Okay, I'm with you, said Breezy. Do we need to pack," she asked. "That's the beauty of it. We can say the magic words over the phone and poof like magic we'll be there.

"Are you ready Breezy?" "Yes. I am so excited" said Breezy. "Then close your eyes, and repeat after me," said Jeniya....

"Wonders elegant to behold,
Starlight shines as bright as the gold,
Fairy mist among the trees,
Take us to our fairy dreams."

After speaking the special magic words, Jeniya and Breezy found themselves in a Forest. All around them were beautiful and colorful trees like they had never seen before. There was beautiful golden dust sprinkled on the rocks and the sound of fairies singing filled the air. "Oh, what a beautiful place this is," said Breezy. I can't believe we made it. Okay, so what do we do now?" "Well, Angel didn't tell me what to do next. I got us here, now you figure out the rest." "Me? How am I supposed to do that? You're the one who knew an official fairy princess! I shouldn't have come with you. You always get me in trouble," said Breezy, folding her arms. "You do a pretty good job of getting yourself in trouble," said Jeniya. "We're just... well, we're just lost!" said Jeniya. "Really... Duh!" responded Breezy as she sat down on a very large rock. Jeniya sat down next to her. "Let's just calm down and try to get our thoughts together," said Jeniya. "Hey, get off of me! Do I look like a chair?"

Jeniya and Breezy jumped so high their heads brushed the leaves on the tree above. "Who said that?" asked Jeniya. "Don't look at me," said Breezy. "I think it came from under us." "Did you say that?" asked Breezy looking at the rock. "Of course I did. You can't just come along sitting on top of rocks in this place. I think I'll report you both to the Fairy Queen." stated the rock. "Okay, <u>now</u> we're in trouble," said Jeniya. Perhaps the Fairy Queen can help us out, she thought. "Hey! Mister talking rock, take us to the Fairy Queen," demanded Jeniya. "Who do you think you are, bossing me around? I am in charge of this forest. And I am placing you both under arrest."

Smaller rocks began to move toward Jeniya and Breezy. They formed a line around the girls. The large rock ordered them to march. So, they marched! "Do you think it's going to take a long time to get where we're going," asked Jeniya. "No talking in formation!" yelled the large rock. "Just keep moving!" Jeniya and Breezy were beginning to wonder if being a fairy princess was worth all this drama. Coming to an opening between the trees, Jeniya and Breezy saw the most beautiful house sitting at the foot of a hill. "Is that where we're going," asked Jeniya. "Yes, that's where we're going," answered the big rock. "Don't be too happy though. Your fate is in the hands of the Fairy Queen. You better hope she's in a good mood." As they approached the door, the rocks stopped marching and the big rock rolled around and knocked on the door. When the door opened it made a creaking sound as if it needed oil. There stood a woman. She had long silver hair that flowed down to the floor. She had on golden slippers and a beautiful scarf drapped around her neck. She wore glasses on the tip of her nose and when she opened the door she smiled the largest smile. "What have we here," she asked. "These two appeared in the forest without permission," replied the rock. "You two don't look dangerous. As a matter of fact you look rather like cute. Are you fairies," asked the woman. "No ma'am. My name is Breezy and this is my cousin Jeniya. We've come all this way because my cousin's friend Angel said this is where you go to become a fairy princess. Please tell me this is the right place."

"Oh, this is the right place all right. Let me introduce myself. My name is Lenora and I am a fairy princess. It's been a long time for me since I wore my crown but I still have my wings. If you want to be fairy princesses, there is much to learn. You must first get permission from the Fairy Queen. Her name is Gisele but you must always address her as Queen Gisele. Can you remember that," asked Lenora" "Yes, I think we can. We will practice until we get it right," replied Breezy. "You must get it right or... well...I won't spoil the fun. Stay here. I'll go in to speak with the Queen. Sir Rock you and your army may go, thank you," announced Lenora. Lenora invited the girls inside and closed the door. She beckoned Jeniya and Breezy to sit down. "Sit here until I return for you and do not move from this spot."

Fairy Princess Lenora disappeared from sight. "Did you see that? She disappeared like magic," said Jeniya. "Well get used to it Jeniya. We are among the fairy princesses now. I'm sure there's a lot of magic going on here," said Breezy. Down a long corridor walked Fairy Princess Lenora. At the end of the hall was a large golden door. Standing guard outside the door were the blue Knights. The blue Knights were responsible for the safety of all who lived in the realm. "I wish a word with Queen Gisele," said Fairy Princess Lenora. The guard opened the door and Princess Lenora entered the room. What a beautiful place. Gold, silver and diamonds were everywhere you could see. A big royal bed sat at the end of the room. And the throne, specifically positioned to face the doorway was covered in red velvet and gold ribbon studded with diamonds. Sitting on the throne was the most heavenly figure. She wore a beautiful white dress with a diamond trimmed veil over her face. Her hands were slender and her nails were polished. Her hair was long and circled her throne. At her side was a crystal wand that glistened in the light coming through the window. In a very soft voice she said, "I understand we have visitors." "Yes ma'am we do. They say Angel sent them to become fairy princesses." The queen sat forward. "Angel? Are you sure they said Angel? Why would Angel tell our secret? She must have thought them worthy of training. I must speak with them immediately. Bring them to me. I'd like to have a look at them," said the Queen. When Fairy Princess Lenora returned she found Jeniya and Breezy fast asleep. They were still sitting where they were ordered to sit. Lenora stood for a moment watching the two girls. They are quite beautiful. They look like fairy princesses. They just need dusting off a bit. I bet with a little work I can turn them into beautiful fairy princesses. I hope Queen Gisele will allow them to stay, she thought. "Wake up my lovelies," said Lenora. It is time to meet your host. There is no time to waste.

Hopefully you girls will get permission to stay and you won't waste my time. Lenora took the two girls down the long corridor to the golden door. The guard immediately let them in closing the door behind them. "You must kneel in the presence of Queen Gisele," ordered Lenora. The two girls kneeled. They were afraid to look up. Breezy noticed she had on the most beautiful shoes. "Who are you? State your name and purpose! You may rise," said Gisele as she sat back on her throne. "Well, my name is Breezy, I mean Brazyl Price. "Is your family royalty," asked Gisele. "I really don't know," answered Breezy. "You may continue" said Gisele. I don't have any sisters and brothers. My mother's name is Angelica. "Okay, who are you," Gisele asked looking at Jeniya. "My name is Jeniya Morton. I have an older sister whose name is Julie. Breezy is my cousin. "My mom's name is Valeria and my father is John." "Jeniya, your mother's name sounds familiar. Are you certain it was Angel who told you about this place," asked the Queen. "I am telling the truth. I hope you believe me because I want to be a fairy princess more than anything in the world," responded Jeniya. "And this is also how you feel, Breezy?" "Oh yes, more than anything in the world." The Queen leaned forward and said, "Okay, I'll have to verify some information about your families and in the meantime you can get started training with Fairy Princess Lenora. You must do everything she tells you. And your first assignment will be deciding what kind fairy you are to become. Leave me and do not disappoint me." Fairy Princess Lenora escorted the two girls back down the corridor. "You see not all fairies are princesses. We may not always wear crowns, but we earn our wings. This you must remember. It is not enough to make me proud. You must make yourself proud." The girls arrived in the kitchen. "Why have we returned to the kitchen," Jeniya asks. "Well, I'm assuming you're hungry but if you're not you may retire to bed." "We are starving! I can really eat something right now, can't you Breezy?" "I definitely can. What do you have to eat," asked Breezy. "My child, I have fairy food. It is what all fairies eat."

After finishing their berries and fruit, the two girls were tired. Fairy Princess Lenora showed them where they would be sleeping. They were too tired to notice how pretty the room was all colored in pink and purple....their favorite colors. They washed their faces and brushed their teeth and slipped softly into bed. Within seconds they were asleep. "Sleep well my lovelies, for tomorrow is a special day," said Lenora as she quietly closed the door.

   The next morning the girls were awaken by a beautiful Fairy
Princess perched on a mushroom. "Good Morning! My name is
Selenia. I am a Tree Fairy. I normally sit on the branches and sing to
the flowers, the butterflies, the frogs, and every living creature in the
forest. You must get dressed. There is much to teach you and we only
have one day." With that, Selenia vanished in thin air. "Wow, you
were right. There is magic all up in here," laughed Jeniya as the girls
ran to get dressed.

"Look, there's a note on the closet door," said Breezy. "What does it say?" asked Jeniya. "Wear the items I left for you at the foot of your beds," sign Fairy Princess Lenora. At the foot of their beds were silky shiny dresses. The girls felt like real fairy princesses when they put them on. Once dressed, the girls headed to the kitchen to eat breakfast.

"**N**o time for sitting this morning. We have much to teach you. Grab some berries and follow me," said Lenora, walking down the corridor. Grabbing the berries, the girls ran to catch up with Lenora. Finally, she stopped at a large blue door. "This is where the training takes place," said Lenora. Hurry in, let's get started." Inside the room were small chairs and small desks. "Sit anywhere lovelies and let us begin," Lenora said. "First thing we need to do is define "fairy." Jeniya you may stand and tell me what your definition of a fairy," said Lenora. Jeniya nervously stood and said, "A fairy is mostly girls and they do special things. They help people and show people the way when they get lost. They are very kind and they love the outside." Lenora smiled, "That was a very good answer Jeniya. You may be seated. Now, Breezy, what is your definition of a fairy?" Breezy stood, took a deep breath and replied, "Well, I think a fairy is different... although your answer Jeniya is really good. But for me, a fairy is about beauty, glittering jewels, pretty dresses and singing. They have golden wings and big beautiful bright smiles. They help people too, but in a different way. At night they listen to the prayers of children and watch over them until as they sleep." Once again, Lenora smiled. "That is a very interesting answer, said Lenora. You both are correct. There are many types of fairies and they all do different things. The one thing they have in common is love.

I asked you this question to determine your gift. True fairies are always gifted something very special. Jeniya, you will be an Earth Fairy. Your spirit is closest to the earth and nature since you love to be outside. Earth Fairies are caring, creative and spectacular. Breezy, you shall be the Jewel Fairy. Your hair is spun of gold dust, braided and tucked inside the braids are diamonds and rubies. You carry beauty to the world. You specifically listen to the prayers of children and leave behind a small amount of beauty for them to keep inside their hearts. I have another question for both of you. Do you feel different," asked Lenora. "Strangely, I do feel different," said Breezy. "I feel different too. Why do we feel this way," asked Jeniya. Lenora smiled and said, "It is because your gift has been awakened inside of you. This doesn't always happen so quickly. This only happens when there are fairies in your family or among your friends back at home. I suspect Angel is the reason. She was right to send you both here," said Lenora. "Would you like to speak with the fairy that is most like you?" she asked. "Yes, please. I would love to speak with her." "So would I," said Breezy. "Good! I will take you to them. There is much to learn." The girls followed Lenora outside. They begin to walk back into the forest.

They came to a waterfall alongside a hill. Lenora picked up a stone and tossed it into the water. The waterfall separated and an entry appeared. "Please come in Breezy. I've been expecting you," said the voice inside. Entering they saw a beautiful Fairy with many jewels and wearing a purple dress. "I am Amethyst, the Jewel Fairy. Please come in and have a seat." They sat on silk pillows and drank morning dew out of buttercups. "May I touch your hair?" asked Amethyst. "I want to see into your heart and pass along the knowledge you need to become a Jewel Fairy," she said. "It would be an honor," replied Breezy moving closer to the Jewel Fairy. "You have a heart of gold. You are strong-willed and independent. Those are qualities that you will find helpful. Now, close your eyes and I will share my knowledge with you through our touch." Breezy closed her eyes. When she finally opened them, everything was different. They were standing outside the waterfall and she felt empowered, strong and happy. "You are smiling like diamonds," said Jeniya. "It is because she is now a Jewel Fairy," said Lenora. "You made it Breezy," said Jeniya. "Not quite," said Lenora. It must be approved by Gisele, the Fairy Princess of them all. Come, we still have to visit the Earth Fairy," said Lenora. At the top of the hill Jeniya saw a large mountain. "Are we going up there?" she asked. "No, we are going inside the mountain," smiled Lenora. You have nothing to fear. We have entered the realm of the Earth Fairy."

"Welcome to my realm ladies. Please come in and get comfortable. Would you like some berries and fruit?" Standing before them was a beautiful fairy. "My name is Oleria and I am the Earth Fairy. Jeniya, please come sit beside me." Everyone sat down. "I love to be outside among all the creatures, but I also love my lair within the realm I have created. The earth is where life begins and it is my responsibly to care for it. Is that something you want to do," she asked Jeniya. "Yes, it is my only dream. I always wanted to be a fairy princess. I never knew there were different types. But, I am happy to know where I belong," she answered. Oleria placed her hand over Jeniya's heart. "Close your eyes, dear Jeniya. Your heart is strong and full of compassion, but you talk back to your mother and you fight at school. There must be no more of that if you are to be an Earth Fairy. Be strong, but use your strength wisely. I pass my knowledge to you, knowing in my heart you will do the right things."

When Jeniya opened her eyes, they were no longer in the realm of the Earth Fairy. "Now it is time to see Queen Gisele, said Lenora. Come, we have only an hour remaining." They traveled the path back to where they started. "You must hurry. Take this leaf and follow me," Lenora said as she handed a long leaf to Jeniya and Breezy. When they approached the golden door, it opened magically. Entering the room they noticed it was full of Fairies. "Come in and stand in front of me," commanded Queen Gisele. You have completed your training and now possess the knowledge you need to become a Fairy. One day, you will meet and marry your Prince. He will give you your crown. It will only be then when you will become princesses. But do not wait for him, for there is much work you must do before he comes along. Hold out the leaf Lenora gave to you." As they held the leaf, each fairy touched the leaf and whispered, "My sister, welcome." When the last fairy had touched the leaf all the fairies vanished in a puff of smoke. Jeniya and Breezy felt very light. Looking around they realized they were floating. "We have wings!" yelled Breezy. "You also have all the powers a fairy of your kind must have, said the Queen. Breezy, I am changing your name to Saphyria, the Jewel Fairy. It is the name you will use among your sister fairies only.

As for you Jeniya, I will not change your name. Your name means of noble origin. You will grow to be responsible in your life away from the realm. Your ability to balance situations will prove to be priceless. You have natural abilities given to you by your parents to help others. You will be known as Jeniya, the Earth Fairy. Do you both understand your responsibilities," asked Queen Gisele. Both girls smiled and replied, "Yes, Queen Gisele. We understand." The Queen took each girls hand and said, "Your time here is running out. You must return home to your families. Remember who you are and what that means. Once you leave the realm, your wings will no longer be visible, but they will still be there. Lenora will lead you to the edge of the realm so that you may return home," said Gisele.

They finally reached the edge of the realm. Lenora picked two golden stones from the ground and placed one in each girl's hand. "To go home you must hold the stones tightly in your left hand and join your right hands together. Now, you must repeat after me:

Blue is the sky above us.
Dark is the night below.
Warm is our hearts with love
To our families we will go."

"Jeniya, get off that phone. You have school tomorrow!" Jeniya opened her eyes to find herself safe at home. "Yes Mom, I'm just saying good night to Breezy," said Jeniya. "Well, Breezy that was quite a trip wasn't it? I still have my stone! Do you have your stone too," asked Jeniya. Breezy looked at her hand. There was her golden stone. "I have my stone too. I am so glad we went together. Do you feel like a Fairy," Breezy asked. "Yes I do!" "Me too," said Breezy. "Good night Jeniya, Earth Fairy." With a big smile on her face Jeniya replied, "Sleep well dear cousin Saphyria, Jewel Fairy. I think I'm going to have a bedtime snack. I have a taste for berries!"

www.ingramcontent.com/pod-product-compliance
Lightning Source LLC
Chambersburg PA
CBHW041536240626
47164CB00002B/35